First published 2021

1st Edition

T-Rex in a Tutu

Written by Bee Bourke
Illustrated by Ella Holden

Once there was a dinosaur named Fred, who loved to dance.

He would whirl and twirl at every chance.

One year for Fred's birthday he got a wonderful gift.

It was soft and squidgy and easy to lift.

Fred tore open the wrapping and to his surprise,

inside was a tutu, in just the right size.

Fred put it on, his eyes wide with delight,

and he twirled, and he whirled in it, all through
the night.

The next day Fred wore his tutu, still twirling with glee,

dancing and grinning for all who could see.

Arriving at school, he spotted his friends. He ran over to Violet, Dylan and Finn,

and displayed his tutu with a pirouette spin.

He looked at their faces as he finished his twirl,

but they sniggered and giggled, and said, 'You're dressed like a girl!'

Fred's smile crumpled; his heart filled with dismay,

he didn't know why his friends would treat him this way.

Fred felt confused and upset and so he trudged into class,

his heart feeling heavy and his features downcast.

He still could hear their sniggers and he tried not to cry,

by turning to the window and heaving a sigh.

His teacher came in
and greeted the
class,

though Fred kept his gaze
outside on the grass.

'Good Morning children, I thought you should know,'

'that today we've been asked to put on a show!'

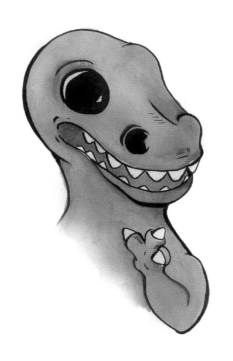

Fred perked himself up at
hearing this news,

perhaps he could dance,
he had nothing to lose.

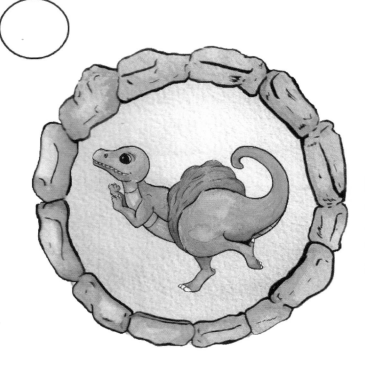

Walking to the hall, he felt his tutu wiggle,

and faintly he heard a laugh and a giggle.

They arrived at the hall and sat facing the stage,

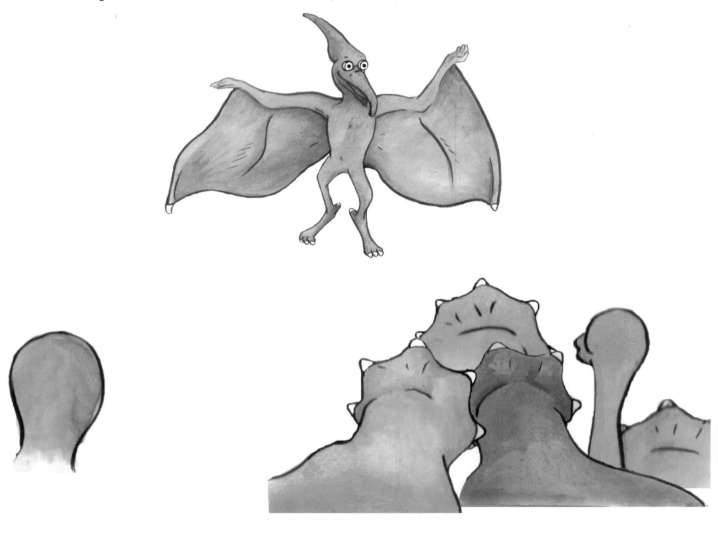

whilst the teacher checked names off, starting
with Paige.

Once the teacher had checked that everyone was there,

they settled themselves on the teacher's chair.

They looked at their class seeing Fred's tearful face,

and how he was alone, surrounded by space.

Then they spotted Fred's tutu and had an idea.

'Let's put on a show! I'll need a volunteer?'

Fred's hand shot up,
he was eager to dance,

to show off his
skills and take up
this chance.

So Fred took to the stage, his tutu firmly in place,

and he began to dance with an eloquent grace.

He twirled and
leapt and spun
through the air,

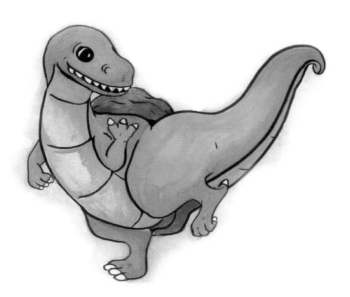

to the gasps of delight
from all watching him
there.

But Fred didn't hear them as he soared over the stage,

his tutu magnificent in the part that it played.

Breathless he finished, his heart feeling light,

to the sounds of applause and obvious delight.

Fred took a bow to
the deafening
sound,

of his friends
cheering loudly and
stomping the
ground.

When Fred had finished and re-joined his friends,

they all started speaking, wishing to make amends.

'We're sorry we laughed and made fun of your skirt,'

'We didn't think of your feelings or how it might hurt.'

'You're such a good dancer, but we never knew,
about dancing skirts and all they could do.'

'It's what ballerinas wear,
and it's called a tutu.'

Fred looked at them all and no longer felt sad,

he said he forgave them, and they all looked quite glad.

'We'd love to try and dance like you.'

'Please could you teach us, in your beautiful tutu?'

Fred smiled wide, his heart
feeling light,

his friends' eager faces were a
wonderful sight.

And so Fred led with a twirl and a plié,

and they continued to practise for the rest of the
day.

Fred was elated now his friends understood,

how much he loved dancing and that they
thought he was good.

T-Rex in a Tutu was written by Bee Bourke and illustrated by Ella Holden.

No dinosaurs were harmed in the making of this book, even when they got dizzy from too much twirling.